THE LITTLE MERMAID

To Simone

—M.H.

Henry Holt and Company, Inc.
Publishers since 1866
115 West 18th Street
New York, New York 10011

Henry Holt is a registered
trademark of Henry Holt and Company, Inc.

Specially edited text
Copyright © 1981 by Henry Holt and Company, Inc.
Story adapted by Jane S. Woodward;
originally appeared in *Michael Hague's Favourite*
Hans Christian Andersen Fairy Tales.
All rights reserved.
Published in Canada by Fitzhenry & Whiteside Ltd.,
195 Allstate Parkway, Markham, Ontario L3R 4T8.

Library of Congress Cataloging-in-Publication Data
Andersen, H. C. (Hans Christian), 1805–1875.
[Lille havfrue. English]
The little mermaid / Hans Christian Andersen;
illustrated by Michael Hague.
Summary: A little sea princess, longing to be human,
trades her mermaid's tail for legs, hoping to win the
love of a prince and earn an immortal soul for herself.
[1. Fairy tales.   2. Mermaids — Fiction.]
I. Hague, Michael, ill.   II. Title.
PZ8.A542Lit   1993   [Fic]—dc20   92-29807
ISBN 0-8050-1010-6

First Edition — 1994

Printed in the United States of America
on acid-free paper. ∞

1 3 5 7 9 10 8 6 4 2

HANS CHRISTIAN ANDERSEN

~ T H E ~

LITTLE MERMAID

Illustrated by M I C H A E L   H A G U E

HENRY HOLT AND COMPANY

New York

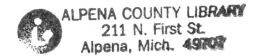

ar out in the ocean the water is as blue as the most beautiful cornflower and as clear as the purest crystal. But it is very deep — much deeper, in fact, than any anchor chain can sound. Many church steeples would have to be piled one on top of the other to reach from the bottom to the surface of the water. Down there live the sea folk.

Now you must not think that there is nothing but bare white sand down at the bottom. No, the strangest trees and plants grow there, with such pliant stems and leaves that at the slightest movement of the water they stir as if they are alive. All the big and little fishes glide in and out among their branches, as the birds do in the trees up above.

Where the ocean is deepest stands the Sea King's palace. Its walls are made of coral, and the high-arched windows of the clearest amber. The roof is made of mussel shells, which open and close in the current. It is very beautiful, for each of them is filled with gleaming pearls, any one of which would make a jewel fit for a queen's crown.

The Sea King had been a widower for many years, but his old mother kept house for him. She was a clever woman, but very vain and proud of her noble rank, so she wore twelve oysters on her tail, while other nobles were only allowed to wear six. In other respects she deserved great praise, especially for her tender care of the little Sea Princesses, her granddaughters. They were six lovely children, and the youngest was the most beautiful of all. Her skin was as clear and delicate as a rose petal, and her eyes as blue as the deepest sea, but, like all the others, she had no legs — her body ended in a fishtail. All day long they used to play in the great halls of the palace, where living flowers grew out of the walls. When the large amber windows were thrown open, the fishes came swimming in to them, as the swallows fly in to us when we open our windows. But the fishes swam right up to the little Princesses, and ate out of their hands, and let themselves be petted and stroked.

In front of the palace was a large garden, in which bright red and dark blue trees were growing. The fruit glittered like gold, and the flowers looked like flames of fire, with their ever-moving stems and leaves. The ground was covered with the finest sand, as blue as burning brimstone. A strange blue light shone over everything, so that one could imagine oneself to be high up in the air, with the blue sky above and below, rather than at the bottom of the sea. When the sea was calm, one could see the sun. It looked like a huge purple flower, from whose center the light streamed forth.

Each of the little Princesses had her own place in the garden, where she could dig and plant as she pleased. One gave her flower bed the shape of a whale; another preferred to make hers like a little mermaid; but the youngest made hers as round as the sun, and only had flowers that shone red like it. She was a strange child, quiet and thoughtful. While her sisters made a great display of all sorts of curious objects that they found from wrecked ships, she only loved her rose-red flowers, like the sun above, and a beautiful marble statue of a handsome boy carved out of clear white stone, which had sunk from some wreck to the bottom of the sea. She had planted by the statue a rose-colored weeping willow, which grew well, with its fresh branches arching over it, down to the blue sand, and casting a violet shadow that moved to and fro like the branches, so that it looked as if the top of the tree and the roots were playing at kissing each other.

Nothing gave her more pleasure than to hear stories about the world of men above. She made her old grandmother tell her all she knew about ships and towns, people and animals. It seemed strangely beautiful to her that on earth the flowers were fragrant, for at the bottom of the sea they have no scent; that the woods were green, and that the fish which one saw there among the branches could sing so loudly and beautifully that it was a delight to hear them. The grandmother called the little birds fishes; otherwise her granddaughters would not have understood her, for they had never seen a bird.

"When you are fifteen years old," said the grandmother, "you will be allowed to go up to the surface of the sea and sit on the rocks in the moonlight, and see the big ships sail by. Then you will also see the forests and towns."

The following year one of the sisters would be fifteen; but the others — well, the sisters were each one year younger than the other; so the youngest had to wait fully five years before she could come up from the bottom of the sea and see what things were like on the earth above. But each promised to tell her sisters what she had seen and liked best on her first day, for their grandmother could not tell them enough — there were so many things they wanted to know.

None of them, however, longed so much to go up as the youngest, who had the longest time to wait, and was so quiet and thoughtful. Many a night she stood at the open window and looked up through the dark blue water, where the fishes splashed with their fins and tails. She could see the moon and the stars, which only shone faintly, but looked much bigger through the water than we see them. When something like a dark cloud passed under them, and hid them for a while, she knew it was either a whale swimming overhead or a ship with many people, who had no idea that a lovely little mermaid was standing below stretching out her white hands toward the keel of their ship.

The eldest Princess was now fifteen years old, and was allowed to rise to the surface of the sea. When she came back she had hundreds of things to tell: but what pleased her most, she said, was to lie in the moonlight on a sandbank, in the calm sea, and to see near the coast the big town where the lights twinkled like hundreds of stars; to hear the music and the noise and bustle of carriages and people, and to see the many church towers and spires and listen to the ringing of the bells.

Oh, how the youngest sister listened to all this! And when, later in the evening, she again stood at the open window, looking up through the dark blue water, she thought of the big town, with all its bustle and noise, and imagined that she too could hear the church bells ringing, even down where she was.

The next year the second sister was allowed to go up to the surface and swim about as she pleased. She came up just as the sun was setting, and this, she thought, was the most beautiful sight of all. The whole sky was like gold, she said, and the clouds—well, she could not find the words to describe their beauty. Rose and violet, they sailed by over her head. But, even swifter than the clouds, a flock of wild swans, like a long white veil, flew across the water toward the sun. She followed them, but the sun sank, and the rosy gleam faded from the clouds and the sea.

The following year the third sister went up. She was the boldest of them all, and she swam up a broad river that flowed into the sea. She saw beautiful green hills covered with vines, and houses and castles peeped out from magnificent forests. She heard the birds sing, and the sun shone so warmly that she often had to dive under the water to cool her burning face. In a little creek she came across a whole flock of little children, who were quite naked and splashed about in the water. She wanted to play with them, but they were frightened and ran away. Then a little black animal — it was a dog, but she had never seen a dog before — came out and barked so ferociously at her that she became frightened and swam quickly back to the open sea. But she could never forget the beautiful forests, the green hills, and the lovely children, who could swim even though they had no fishtails.

The fourth sister was not so daring. She stayed far out in the open sea, and said that was the loveliest place of all. There, she said, one could see for many miles around, and the sky above was like a great glass dome. She saw ships, but far away, and they looked to her like seagulls. The playful dolphins, she said, turned somersaults, and the big whales spewed out seawater through their spouts, as if a hundred fountains were playing all around her.

Now the fifth sister's turn came, and, as her birthday was in winter, she saw things on her first visit that the other sisters had not. The sea looked quite green; huge icebergs floated around her — they were like pearls, she said, and yet were much higher than the church steeples built by men. They were the strangest shapes and glittered like diamonds. She sat on one of the biggest, and all the passing sailors were terrified when they saw her sitting there, with the wind playing with her long hair. Toward evening the sky became overcast with black clouds; there were thunder and lightning, and the dark waves lifted up the big blocks of ice, which shone in each flash of lightning. On all the ships the sails were furled, and the men were filled with anxiety and terror. But she sat quietly on her floating iceberg and watched the blue lightning dart in zigzags into the foaming sea.

The first time each one of the sisters came to the surface all the new and beautiful things she saw charmed her. But now, when as grown-up girls they were allowed to come up whenever they liked, they soon ceased to marvel at the upper world and longed for their home; and after a month they said that after all it really was best down below, where one felt at home. On many an evening the five sisters would rise to the surface of the sea, arm in arm. They had beautiful voices, far finer than those of any human being; and when a storm was brewing, and they thought that some ships might be wrecked, they swam in front of them, singing so beautifully of how lovely it was at the bottom of the sea, and telling the sailors not to be afraid to come down to them. But the sailors could not understand the words and thought it was only the noise of the storm; and they never saw the wonders below, for when the ship went down they were drowned, and were dead when they came to the Sea King's palace.

When her sisters went up arm in arm to the top of the sea there stood the little sister, all alone, looking after them, and feeling as if she wanted to cry. But mermaids have no tears, and so they suffer all the more.

"Oh, if I were only fifteen!" she said. "I know how much I shall love the world above, and the people who live in it."

At last she reached her fifteenth birthday.

"Well, now we have you off our hands," said her grandmother, the old dowager queen. "Come now! Let me dress you like your sisters!" She put a wreath of white lilies in her hair, but every petal of the flowers was half a pearl; and the old lady put eight big oysters on the Princess's tail, to show her high rank.

"But it hurts!" said the little mermaid.

"Yes, but one must suffer to be beautiful," said the old lady.

Oh, how gladly the little Princess would have taken off all her ornaments and the heavy wreath! The red flowers in her garden would have suited her much better, but she dared not make any

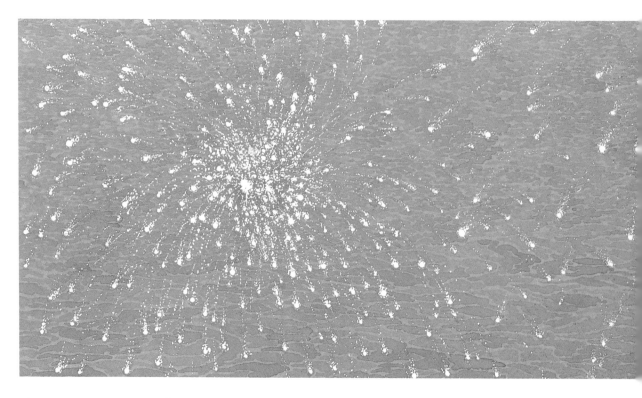

change now. "Good-bye!" she said, and rose as lightly as a bubble through the water.

The sun had just set when she lifted her head out of the water, but the clouds gleamed with red and gold, and the evening star shone brightly in the rosy sky. The air was mild and fresh, and the sea as calm as glass. Near her lay a big ship with three masts. Only one sail was set, as not a breath of wind was stirring, and the sailors were sitting about on deck and in the rigging. There was music and singing on board, and when it grew dark many hundreds of colored lamps were lighted, and it looked as if the flags of all nations were floating in the air. The little mermaid swam close to the cabin windows, and when the waves lifted her up she could see through the clear panes many richly dressed people. But the handsomest of them all was the young Prince, with large black eyes. He could not have been more than sixteen. In fact, it was his birthday that was being celebrated. The sailors were dancing on deck, and when the young Prince came

out hundreds of rockets rose into the air, making the night as bright as day, so that the little mermaid was frightened, and dived underwater. But soon she raised her head again, and then it seemed to her as if all the stars of heaven were falling down upon her. Never had she seen such fireworks! Great suns whirled around, wondrous fiery fish flew through the blue air, and everything was reflected in the clear, calm sea. The ship was so brilliantly lit up that one could see everything distinctly, even to the smallest rope, and the people still better. Oh, how handsome the young Prince was! He shook hands with the people and smiled graciously, while the music drifted through the starry night.

It grew very late, but the little mermaid could not tear her eyes away from the ship and the handsome Prince. The colored lamps were put out, no more rockets were sent up nor cannons fired. But deep down in the sea was a strange moaning and murmuring, and the little mermaid sitting on the waves was rocked up and down, so that

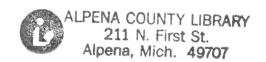

she could look into the cabin. Soon the ship began to move faster, as one sail after another was unfurled. Then the waves rose higher and higher, dark clouds gathered, and flashes of lightning were seen in the distance. Oh, what a terrible storm was brewing! Then the sailors reefed all the sails, and the big ship plunged wildly through the raging sea. The waves rose as high as great black mountains, as if they would dash over the masts, but the ship dived like a swan between them, and then was carried up again to their towering crests. The little mermaid thought this was great fun, but not the sailors. The ship creaked and groaned, her strong timbers gave way under the weight of the huge waves, the sea broke over her; the mainmast snapped in two, like a reed; and the ship heeled over on her side while the water rushed into her hold.

The little mermaid realized that the crew was in danger. She herself had to be careful of the beams and planks floating about in the water. For a moment it was so dark that nothing could be seen, but then flashes of lightning made everything visible, and she could see

all on board. The little mermaid looked for the young Prince, and as the ship broke up she saw him sinking into the depths of the sea. At first she was very pleased, for now he would come down and live with her; but then she remembered that men cannot live in the water, and only if he were dead could he come to her father's palace. No, no, he must not die! Heedless of the beams and planks floating on the water, which could have crushed her, she dived down into the water and came up again in the waves, searching for the Prince. At last she found him. His strength was failing him, and he could hardly swim any longer in the raging sea. His arms and legs began to grow numb, and his beautiful eyes closed. He would certainly have died if the little mermaid had not come to his aid. She held his head above water and let the waves carry them where they would.

Next morning the storm was over, but not a plank of the ship was to be seen anywhere. The sun rose red and brilliant out of the water and seemed to bring new life to the Prince's cheeks, but his eyes remained closed. The little mermaid kissed his beautiful high fore-

head, and smoothed back his wet hair. She thought he looked very much like the white marble statue in her little garden. She kissed him again and again, and prayed that he might live.

Then she saw before her eyes the mainland with its high, blue mountains on whose summits snow was glistening, so that they looked like swans. Along the shore were beautiful green woods, and in front of them stood a church or convent — she did not know which, but it was some sort of building. Lemon trees and orange trees grew in the garden, and before the gate stood lofty palm trees. The sea formed a little bay here and was quite calm, though very deep. She swam straight to the cliffs, where the fine white sand had been washed ashore, and laid the handsome Prince on the sand, taking care that his head should lie in the warm sunshine.

Then all the bells began to ring in the big white building, and many young girls came out into the garden. The little mermaid swam out and hid behind some rocks, covering her hair and breast with sea foam, to make sure no one could see her face, and from there she watched to see who would come to find the poor Prince.

Before long a young girl came to the spot where he lay. At first she seemed very frightened, but only for a moment, then she called to some of the others. The little mermaid saw that the Prince came back

to life, and smiled at all who stood around him. But he did not smile at her, for he did not know who had saved him. She was very sad; and when they had taken him into the big building, she dived down into the water and went back to her father's palace.

She had always been silent and thoughtful, and now she became even more so. Her sisters asked her what she had seen up above for the first time, but she told them nothing. Many a morning and many an evening she went back to the place where she had left the Prince. She saw how the fruit in the garden ripened and was gathered, and how the snow melted on the high mountains, but she never saw the Prince, and each time she returned home she was more unhappy than before.

Her only comfort was to sit in her little garden and put her arms around the marble figure which was so like the Prince. She no longer looked after her flowers. Her garden became a wilderness; the plants straggled over the paths and twined their long stalks and leaves around the branches of the trees, so that it became quite dark and gloomy there.

At last she could bear it no longer, and confided her troubles to one of her sisters, who, of course, told the others. These and a few other mermaids, who also told their intimate friends, were the only people who were in on the secret. One of them knew who the Prince was. She too had watched the festivities on board the ship, and could tell them where his kingdom lay.

"Come, little sister!" said the other Princesses, and linking arms, they rose to the surface of the sea, to where the Prince's palace stood. It was built of pale yellow stone, and had broad marble staircases, one of which reached right down to the sea. Magnificent gilt cupolas surmounted the roof, and in the colonnades, which ran all around the building, stood lifelike marble statues. Through the clear panes of the high windows could be seen stately halls, hung with costly silk curtains and beautiful tapestries, and on all the walls were beautiful paintings. In the center of the largest hall a big fountain was playing.

Its jets rose as high as the glass dome in the ceiling, through which the sun shone on the water and on the lovely plants that grew in the great basin.

Now she knew where he lived, and many an evening and many a night she returned there. She swam much closer to the shore than any of the others had ventured, and she even went up the narrow

channel under the magnificent marble balcony that cast a long shadow over the water. There she would sit and gaze at the young Prince, who thought that he was all alone in the bright moonlight.

Many an evening she saw him sailing in his stately boat, with the music on board and flags waving. She watched from behind the green rushes, and when the wind caught her long silvery white veil, and people saw it, they thought it was only a swan spreading its wings. At night, when the fishermen were out casting their nets by lamplight, she heard them say many kind things about the Prince, and she was glad that she had saved his life when he was drifting half-dead on the waves. She remembered how heavily his head had lain upon her breast, and how lovingly she had kissed him, but he knew nothing of this, and did not even see her in his dreams.

Daily her love for human beings increased, and more and more she longed to be able to live among them, for their world seemed to her so much bigger than hers. They could sail over the sea in great ships and climb mountains higher than the clouds, and the lands they owned stretched out, in woods and fields, farther than her eyes could see. There were still so many things she wanted to know about, and as her sisters could not answer all her questions, she asked her grand-mother, who knew the upper world very well, and rightly called it "the countries above the sea."

"If human beings are not drowned," asked the little mermaid, "can they live forever? Don't they die as we do down here in the sea?"

"Yes," said the old lady, "they also die, and their life is even shorter than ours. We can live to be three hundred, but when we cease to exist we are turned into foam on the water, and do not even have a grave down here among our loved ones. We do not have immortal souls, and can never live again. We are like the green rushes, which, when once cut down, can never grow again. Human beings, however, have a soul that lives forever, even after the body has turned to dust. It rises through the clear air up to the shining stars. As we rise out of the water and see all the countries of the earth, so they rise to unknown, beautiful regions which we shall never see."

"Why don't we also have an immortal soul?" said the little mermaid sorrowfully. "I would gladly give all the hundreds of years I have yet to live if I could only be a human being for one day, and afterwards have a share in the heavenly kingdom."

"You must not think of that," said the old lady. "We are much happier and better off than the human beings up there."

"So I must die, and float as foam on the sea, and never hear the

music of the waves or see the beautiful flowers and the red sun! Is there nothing I can do to win an immortal soul?"

"No," said the grandmother. "Only if a man loved you so much that you were dearer to him than father or mother, and if he clung to you with all his heart and all his love, and let the priest place his right hand in yours, with the promise to be faithful to you here and for all eternity — then would his soul flow into your body, and you would receive a share in the happiness of mankind. He would give you a soul and still keep his own. But that can never happen! What is thought most beautiful here below, your fishtail, they would consider ugly on earth — they do not know any better. Up there one must have two clumsy props, which they call legs, in order to be beautiful."

The little mermaid sighed and looked sadly at her fishtail.

"Let us be happy!" said the old lady. "Let us hop and skip through

the three hundred years of our life! That is surely long enough! And afterwards we can rest all the better in our graves. This evening there is to be a Court ball."

It was a magnificent sight; one such has never been seen on earth. The walls and ceiling of the big ballroom were of thick but transparent glass. Several hundred huge mussel shells, some red and others green as grass, stood in rows down the sides, holding blue flames, which illuminated the whole room and shone through the walls, so that the sea outside was brightly lit up. One could see countless fish, both big and small, swimming outside the glass walls; some with gleaming purple scales and others glittering like silver and gold. Through the middle of the ballroom flowed a broad stream, in which the mermen and mermaids danced to their own beautiful singing. No human beings have such lovely voices. The little mermaid sang most

sweetly of all, and they all applauded her. For a moment she felt joyful at heart at the thought that she had the most beautiful voice on land or in the sea. But soon her thoughts returned to the world above, for she could not forget the handsome Prince and her sorrow at not possessing an immortal soul like his. So she stole out of her father's palace, while inside joy and merriment reigned, and sat sorrowfully in her little garden.

Suddenly she heard the sound of a horn through the water, and thought: "Now he is sailing above, he whom I love more than father or mother, and into whose hands I would entrust my life's happiness. I would risk anything to win him and an immortal soul. While my sisters are dancing in my father's palace I will go to the sea witch, whom I have always feared so much. Perhaps she may be able to give me advice and help."

Then the little mermaid left her garden, and went out toward the roaring whirlpools where the witch lived. She had never been that way before: no flowers, no seaweed even, were growing there — only bare, gray sand stretching to the whirlpools, where the currents swirled around like rushing mill wheels, dragging everything with them down into the depths. She had to pass through these dreadful whirlpools to reach the witch's territory. For a long way the only path led over hot bubbling mud, that the witch called the peat bog. Behind it her house stood, in a strange forest, for all the trees and bushes were polyps — half-animal and half-plant — which looked like hundred-headed snakes growing out of the ground. The branches had slimy arms with fingers like wriggling worms, and they moved joint by joint from the root to the topmost branch. Everything that they could lay hold of in the sea they grabbed and held fast, and

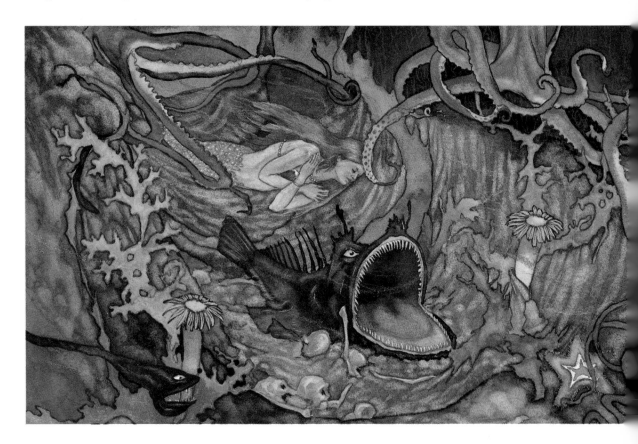

never let it go again. The little mermaid stopped timidly in front of them. Her heart was pounding with fear, and she almost turned back. But then she thought of the Prince and of man's immortal soul, and took courage. She twisted her long flowing hair around her head, in case the polyps should try to seize her by it, and, crossing her hands on her breast, darted through the water as fast as a fish, right past the hideous polyps, who stretched out their writhing arms and fingers after her. She saw that each one of them had seized something, and held it tightly with hundreds of little arms like bands of iron. The bleached bones of men who had perished at sea and sunk into the depths were tightly grasped in the arms of some, while others clutched ships' rudders and sea chests, skeletons of land animals, and — the most terrifying sight of all to her — a little mermaid whom they had caught and strangled.

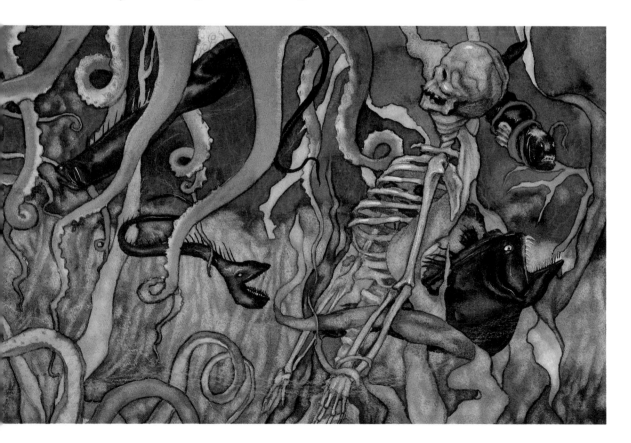

She came to a big slimy place in the forest, where big, fat water snakes were writhing about, showing their ugly yellow bellies. In the middle of this marsh stood a house built of the white bones of shipwrecked men, and there sat the sea witch, letting a toad eat out of her mouth, as we would feed a canary with sugar. The ugly, fat water snakes she called her little chickens, and allowed them to crawl all over her hideous bosom.

"I know exactly what you want!" said the sea witch. "It is stupid of you! But you shall have your way, for it is sure to bring you misfortune, my pretty Princess! You want to get rid of your fishtail and have, instead, two stumps that human beings use for walking, so that the young Prince may fall in love with you, and you may win him and an immortal soul!" As she said this the old witch laughed so loudly and horribly that the toad and snakes fell to the ground, where they lay wriggling. "You have come just in time," said the witch, "for if you had come after sunrise tomorrow I would not have been able to help you for another year. I will make you a potion, and before sunrise you must swim ashore and sit on the be_____ _____ _____ ____

your tail will split in two and shrink into what human beings call legs. But I warn you it will hurt, as if a sharp sword were running through you. Everyone who sees you will say that you are the most beautiful child they have ever seen. You will keep your gracefulness, and no dancer will be able to move as lightly as you. But every step you take will be as painful as treading on a sharp knife. Are you willing to suffer all this, and shall I help you?"

"Yes," said the little mermaid in a trembling voice, and she thought of the Prince and the immortal soul.

"But remember!" said the witch. "When once you have taken the human form you can never become a mermaid again. You will never again be able to dive down through the water to your sisters and your father's palace. And if you fail to win the Prince's love, so that for your sake he will forget father and mother, and cling to you with body and soul, and make the priest join your hands as man and wife, you will not be given an immortal soul. On the first morning after he has married another, your heart will break, and you will turn into foam on the water."

"I will do it," said the little mermaid, as pale as death.

"But you must pay me," said the witch, "and it is not a trifle I ask. You have the most beautiful voice of all who live at the bottom of the sea, and you probably think you can charm the Prince with it — but this voice you must give to me. I must have the best thing you possess in return for my precious drink, for I have to give you my own blood in it, so that the drink may be as sharp as a two-edged sword."

"But if you take away my voice," said the little mermaid, "what have I got left?"

"Your lovely figure," said the witch, "your grace of movement, and your eloquent eyes! With these you can surely capture a human heart. Well, have you lost your courage? Put out your little tongue, so that I may cut it off in payment, and you shall have my magic potion."

"Go ahead," said the little mermaid, and the witch put her cauldron on the fire to prepare the magic drink. "Cleanliness is a good thing," she said, and scoured the cauldron with snakes, which she had tied into a bundle. Then she pricked her breast and let her black blood drip into it, and the steam rose up in the weirdest shapes, so that the little mermaid was frightened and horrified. Every moment the witch threw some new ingredient into the cauldron, and when it boiled the sound was like a crocodile weeping. At last the drink was ready, and it looked like the purest water.

"Here it is!" said the witch, and she cut off the little mermaid's tongue, so that now she was dumb and could neither sing nor speak. "If the polyps should catch hold of you on your way back through my

The little mermaid had no need to do this, however, for the polyps shrank back from her in terror at the sight of the sparkling drink, which gleamed in her hand like a glittering star. So she made her way quickly through the forest and the bog and the roaring whirlpools. She could see her father's palace: in the ballroom the lamps were all out and everyone was asleep, but she dared not go in to see them, now that she was dumb and about to leave them forever. She felt as if her heart would break with sorrow. She stole into the garden, took a flower from each of her sisters' flower beds, blew a thousand kisses to the palace, and then swam up through the dark blue sea.

The sun had not yet risen when she came in sight of the Prince's palace and reached the magnificent marble steps. The moon was shining bright and clear. The little mermaid drank the sharp, burning

draught, and it felt as if a two-edged sword went through her tender body; she fainted, and lay as if dead.

When the sun shone over the sea she awoke, and felt a stabbing pain, but there before her stood the beautiful young Prince. He fixed his black eyes on her, so that she cast hers down and saw that her fishtail had disappeared, and that she now had the prettiest little white legs that any girl could wish for. She was quite naked, though, so she wrapped herself in her long, thick hair. The Prince asked her who she was and how she came to be there, and she looked at him tenderly and sadly with her deep blue eyes, for she could not speak. Then he took her by the hand and led her into the palace. Every step she took, as the witch had warned, was like walking on pointed needles and sharp knives, but she bore it gladly, and walked as lightly as a soap bubble by the side of the Prince, who, with all the others, admired her graceful movement.

They dressed her in costly silk and muslin, and she was the greatest beauty in the palace; but she was dumb, and unable either to sing

sing far more beautifully; and she thought, "Oh, if only he knew that I have given away my voice forever to be with him!"

Now the slaves began to dance light, graceful dances to the loveliest music; and then the little mermaid lifted her beautiful white arms, rose on her toes, and glided across the floor, dancing as no one had ever danced before. At every movement her beauty seemed to grow, and her eyes spoke more deeply to the heart than the songs of the slave girls. Everyone was charmed by her, especially the Prince, who called her his little foundling, and she danced again and again, although every time her feet touched the ground she felt as if she were treading on sharp knives. The Prince said that she should always be near him, and let her sleep on a velvet cushion just outside his door.

He had a page's dress made for her, so that she could ride with him. They rode through sweet-smelling woods, where the green branches brushed her shoulders and the little birds sang among the fresh leaves. With the Prince she climbed the high mountains, and, though her tender feet bled so that all could see it, she smiled and followed him, till they saw the clouds sailing beneath them, like a flock of birds flying to foreign lands.

At home, in the Prince's palace, when all the others were asleep at night, she would go out onto the broad marble steps. It cooled her burning feet to stand in the cold seawater, and then she thought of those she had left down below in the deep.

One night her sisters came up arm in arm, singing sorrowfully as they swam through the water, and she beckoned to them, and they recognized her and told her how sad she had made them all. After that they came to see her every night, and one night she saw, far out to sea, her old grandmother, who had not been up to the surface for many, many years, and the Sea King, with his crown on his head. They stretched out their hands toward her, but did not venture as close to land as her sisters.

"Don't you love me more than all of them?" the little mermaid's eyes seemed to say when the Prince took her in his arms and kissed her beautiful forehead.

"Yes, you are dearest to me," he said, "for you have the best heart of them all. You are the most devoted to me, and you are like a young girl whom I once saw, but whom I fear I shall never meet again. I was on a ship that was wrecked, and the waves washed me ashore near a holy temple where several young maidens were serving in attendance. The youngest of them found me on the beach and saved my life. I only saw her twice. She is the only girl in the world I could love, but you are very much like her, and you almost drive her image from my heart. She belongs to the holy temple, and so by good fortune you have been sent to me, and we shall never part."

"Alas! He doesn't know it was I who saved his life!" thought the little mermaid. "I carried him across the sea to the wood where the temple stands, and I was hidden in the foam, watching to see if anyone would come to him. I saw the beautiful girl whom he loves better than me." She sighed deeply, for she could not weep. "The girl belongs to the holy temple, he says. She will never come out into the world, and they will never meet again. But I am with him and see him every day. I will care for him, love him, and give up my life for him."

But soon the rumor spread that the Prince was to marry the beautiful daughter of a neighboring king, and that was why they were fitting up such a magnificent ship. The Prince is going to visit the neighboring king's country, they said, but everyone knows he is really going to see his daughter. A large suite was to accompany him. The little mermaid shook her head and smiled, for she knew the Prince's thoughts much better than the others. "I must go," he said to her. "I must see the beautiful princess, for my parents wish it; but they will not force me to bring her home as my bride. I cannot love her: she will not be like the beautiful girl in the temple whom you are like. If one day I were to choose a bride I would rather have you, my dumb foundling with the eloquent eyes." And he kissed her red lips, and played with her long hair, and laid his head on her heart, so that she began to dream of human happiness and an immortal soul.

"You are surely not afraid of the sea, my silent child?" he said to her, when they were standing on board the state ship that was to carry him to the neighboring king's country. He told her of the storm and of the calm, of the strange fish in the deep, and of the marvelous things that divers had seen down there, and she smiled at his words,

for she knew more about the things at the bottom of the sea than anyone on earth.

At night, in the bright moonlight, when everyone was asleep except the man at the helm, she sat by the ship's rail, gazing down into the clear water, and thought she could see her father's palace, and her grandmother, with her silver crown on her head, looking up through the swirling currents at the ship's keel. Then her sisters came up out of the water, looking sorrowfully at her and wringing their white hands. She beckoned to them, and smiled, and wanted to tell them that she was well and happy, but a cabin boy came up to her, and her sisters dived under, so that he thought it was just foam on the sea.

The next morning the ship reached the harbor of the neighboring king's beautiful city. All the church bells were ringing, and from the high towers trumpets sounded, while soldiers paraded with flying colors and glittering bayonets. Every day there were festivities; balls and receptions followed one another, but the princess had not yet arrived. She was in a holy convent far away, they said, where she was learning every royal virtue. At last she came. The little mermaid was anxious to see her beauty, and she had to admit that she had never seen anyone lovelier. Her skin was clear and delicate, and behind her long dark lashes smiled a pair of deep blue, loyal eyes.

"You are she!" said the Prince. "She who saved me when I lay

breaking: his wedding morning, she knew, would bring her death, and she would turn into foam on the sea.

The church bells pealed and heralds rode through the streets announcing the betrothal. On all the altars scented oil was burning in costly silver lamps. The priests swung their censers, and the bride and bridegroom joined hands and received the bishop's blessing. The little mermaid, dressed in silk and gold, stood holding the bride's train, but her ears did not hear the joyous music, and her eyes saw nothing of the sacred ceremony — she was thinking of her death, and of all that she had lost in this world.

That same evening the bride and bridegroom came on board the ship; cannons thundered, flags were waved, and in the middle of the ship was erected a royal tent of purple and gold, with the most magnificent couch, where the bridal pair were to rest through the still, cool night.

The sails swelled in the wind, and the ship glided smoothly and almost without motion over the clear sea. When it grew dark colored lamps were lighted, and the sailors danced merrily on deck. The little mermaid could not help thinking of the first time she had risen to the surface and had seen the same splendor and revelry. She threw herself among the dancers, darting and turning as a swallow turns when it is pursued, and they all applauded her, for she had never danced so beautifully before. It was like sharp knives cutting her tender feet, but she did not feel it, for the pain in her heart was much greater. She knew that it was the last evening that she would be with him — him for whom she had left her family and her home, sacrificed her lovely voice, and daily suffered endless pain, of which he knew nothing. It was the last night that she would breathe the same air as he, and see the deep sea and the starry sky. An eternal, dreamless night was waiting for her who had no soul and could not win one. On board the ship the merrymaking lasted till long past midnight, and she laughed and danced with the thought of death in her heart. The

Prince kissed his beautiful bride, and she played with his dark hair, and arm in arm they retired to rest in the magnificent tent.

Everything grew quiet on board; only the steersman stood at the helm. The little mermaid laid her white arms on the rail and looked toward the east for the rosy glimmer of dawn, for she knew that the first sunbeam would kill her.

Then she saw her sisters rising out of the waves; they were as pale as she was, and their beautiful hair no longer floated in the wind, for it had been cut off. "We have given it to the witch, to get her help, so that you will not die tonight. She has given us a knife: here it is. See how sharp it is! Before the sun rises you must thrust it into the Prince's heart, and when the warm blood sprinkles your feet they will grow together again into a fishtail. Then you will be a mermaid again,

and you can come down with us into the sea, and live your three hundred years before you turn into sea foam. Hurry! For he or you must die before sunrise. Our old grandmother is so full of grief for you that her white hair has all fallen out, as ours fell under the witch's scissors. Kill the Prince and come back to us! Hurry! Do you see that red streak in the sky? In a few moments the sun will rise, and then you must die!" They gave a deep sigh and disappeared beneath the

murmured his bride's name in his dreams. Yes, she alone was in his thoughts, and for a moment the knife trembled in the little mermaid's hand. But suddenly she flung it far out into the waves: they shone red when the knife fell, so that it looked as if drops of blood were splashing up out of the water. Once more she looked with dimmed eyes at the Prince, then threw herself from the ship into the sea, and felt her body dissolving into foam.

Now the sun rose out of the sea and its rays fell with gentleness and warmth on the deathly cold sea foam, and the little mermaid felt no pain of death. She saw the bright sun and, floating above her,

hundreds of beautiful transparent beings, through whom she could see the white sails of the ship and the red clouds in the sky. Their melodious voices were so ethereal that no human ear could hear them, just as no earthly eye could see them, and without wings they floated through the air. The little mermaid saw that she had a body like theirs and was slowly rising up out of the foam.

"Where am I going?" she asked, and her voice sounded like that of the other spirits — so ethereal that no earthly music was like it.

"To the daughters of the air," answered the others. "Mermaids have no immortal soul, and can never have one unless they win the

love of a human being. Their eternal life must depend on the power of another. The daughters of the air have no immortal soul either, but by their own good deeds they can win one for themselves. We fly to the hot countries where the pestilent winds kill human beings, and we bring them cool breezes. We spread the fragrance of the flowers through the air, and bring life and healing. When for three hundred years we have striven to do all the good we can, we are given an immortal soul and share the eternal happiness of mankind. You, poor little mermaid, have struggled with all your heart for the same goal, and have suffered and endured. Now you have risen to the spiritual world, and after three hundred years of good deeds you can win an immortal soul for yourself."

And the little mermaid lifted her eyes to the sun, and for the first time she felt tears in them.

On the ship there was life and noise once more. She saw the Prince and his beautiful bride looking for her, and gazing sadly at the gleaming foam, as if they knew that she had thrown herself into the waves. Unseen, she kissed the bride's forehead and smiled at the Prince. Then she rose with the other children of the air up to the rosy clouds that sailed across the sky.

"In three hundred years we shall float like this into the kingdom of God!"

"But we may get there sooner!" whispered one of them. "Unseen,